WEIRD
THROWING
AND KICKING
SPORTS

By S.B. Watson

The Child's World

Published by The Child's World®
1980 Lookout Drive
Mankato, MN 56003-1705
800-599-READ
www.childsworld.com

The Child's World®: Mary Berendes, Publishing Director
The Design Lab: Design and production

Photo credits:
Cover: iStock (top and right); AP/Wide World (left)
Interior: AP/Wide World: 13, 17, 18; Steve Barnett: 10;
Corbis: 14; iStock: 5, 6 top, 8; Press-Register: 6 bottom; Ronn
Murray Photography: 21, 22

Library of Congress Cataloging-in-Publication Data
Watson, S. B.
  Weird throwing and kicking sports / by S. B. Watson.
    p. cm.
  Includes bibliographical references and index.
  ISBN 978-1-60954-379-2 (library reinforced: alk. paper)
  1. Sports for children—Juvenile literature. I. Title.
  GV709.2.W38 2011
  796.083—dc22   2010044026

Printed in the United States of America
Mankato, Minnesota
December, 2010
PA02070

Above: How high can folks throw someone with a walrus skin? Find out on page 22.

For more information about the photo on page 1, turn to page 16.

TABLE OF CONTENTS

People throw mullets like this one. Find out why on page 6.

Hands and Feet

Just about every sport is played using the hands or feet. Most sports use some kind of ball, too. But not every throwing or kicking sport uses a ball. That's where this book comes in. Some of the world's weirdest sports involve throwing everything from a fish to a telephone pole. Others include kicking a ball that's over your head or wrestling with your toes. So **limber** up and throw yourself into this book—just for kicks!

You need your hands (or feet) for football, soccer, and basketball . . . but those sports aren't in this book!

THROW-AWAY FACT!

The most famous mullet toss is held on a beach where Florida and Alabama meet. The event is called the Interstate Mullet Toss, since the fish fly from one state to the other!

A simple mullet (above) becomes a missile in the hand of an expert mullet-tosser.

Fling That Fish!

Mullet tossing is simple. Grab a mullet from the bucket and see how far you can throw it. A mullet is a fish native to the southern United States. A thrower stands at a line in the sand and throws a mullet as far as possible. The longest toss wins. Some players grab their fish by the tail and heave it underhanded like a softball pitcher. Others fold their fish in half or roll it into a ball (ewww). They throw it overhand like a football quarterback. The world mullet-tossing record is 189 feet, 8 inches (58 meters), set by Josh Serotum in 2004.

Throw That Pole!

The caber (KAY-ber) toss is a traditional event in Scotland. A caber is a large wooden pole, like a telephone pole. Tossers have to throw the caber so that it falls directly away from them in a sort of flipping motion. A perfect throw lands with the top end of the pole nearest to the thrower and the bottom end (the end the thrower was holding) pointing exactly away. It takes strength, balance, and the ability to wear a **kilt**.

A caber tosser gets a running start and then tries to flip the caber over.

TOE-TALLY AWESOME FACT!

In 1997, some people who organize toe wrestling tried to get the sport included in the Olympics. Unfortunately, it was not accepted.

Pin That Foot!

In the weird sport of toe wrestling, players lock toes and try to **pin** their opponent's foot. This sport is a lot like thumb wrestling or arm wrestling, but with your feet. Barefoot opponents lock their toes together. The object is to force their opponent's foot to the ground, like arm wrestling. Top players include Paul Beech, known as the "Toeminator."

These feet are ready to go toe-to-toe to find out who is the champion.

Volleyball... With No Hands!

The ball flies back and forth over the net. Players on each team keep the ball in the air, passing or setting up a powerful spike. Is this volleyball? Well, yes—but with a twist. Players can't use their hands. Sepak takraw (SEE-pak TAHK-raw) is also known as kick volleyball. It's very popular in Malaysia and Thailand. Players may only use their feet, knees, chest, and head to touch the ball. This sport is a mix of soccer and volleyball. The best players can kick a ball that's more than seven feet (3.1 m) above the ground!

Players try to "spike" the ball over the net as in volleyball . . . but with their feet!

A sepak takraw ball used to be made from a palm or bamboo plant. Today, it's made of plastic and is smaller than a standard volleyball.

Don't Try to Skip These Stones!

Stone-tossing is a sport? It is in Switzerland. Swiss people have been tossing heavy stones since the 1200s. The men who play this sport toss stones that weigh 138 pounds (63 kg). Women throw rocks that are 75 pounds (34 kg) each! The world record was set by Kevin Marx of Toledo, Ohio, in 2009. He threw his stone 15 feet, 3½ inches (4.7 meters). The women's record of 12 feet, 11 inches (3.9) was set in 2007 by Becky Ball of Marblehead, Ohio.

This Swiss stone-tosser uses an overhand move to send the stone flying . . . sort of.

High Kicks in the Far North

The next few unusual sports all come from the World Eskimo Indian Olympics (WEIO). The WEIO features traditional Native games and sports. Most of these games were inspired by survival skills for life in the rugged Far North. Today, the games are held in a gym, not on the ice. The first sports are high kicks. In the one-foot high kick, the kicker jumps off the floor using both feet. He or she tries to kick a hanging ball with one foot before landing . . . on the kicking foot! The two-foot high jump is similar—kick the ball with both feet and then land with both feet at the same time.

This young man is showing his skill in the two-foot jump, reaching up with all his toes!

The highest one-foot high kick came in 1996. Brian Randazzo touched a ball 9 feet, 6 inches (2.9 m) above the ground.

KICKIN' FACT!

Like other Alaskan Inuit sports, the High Kick developed as a way to teach balance, strength, and endurance—which people needed to survive the harsh Alaskan climate.

It's All About Balance

The Alaska High Kick combines strength and balance. The athlete sits on the floor below a hanging ball. Then the kicker grabs his or her left foot with the opposite hand. With the other hand planted on the floor, the athlete springs up. The player pushes off with the hand, and attempts to kick the ball with one foot. After kicking the object, the athlete must land back on the spot where he or she started. Whoever jumps the highest wins.

The jumper has to keep the non-kicking foot in her hand all the way through the event.

Baby Steps Across the Ice

In this Canadian Eskimo game, players stand at a line with their toes against a small stick. The players keep their feet together while jumping over a stick. It sounds easy, but while the players are in the air, they must kick the stick backward, using the toes of both feet. Players must then land in front of the spot where the stick started. The stick is moved two inches further away from the players' toes until only one player can make the leap successfully.

Toe-kickers need balance and great leaping ability.

22

Look! Up in the Air!

The odd sport of nalakatuk (nah-LAH-kah-took) seems like a simple children's beach game. Actually, it takes strength and skill. One person sits on a blanket held by a group of people. The people fling the blanket up together, and the blanket-rider goes flying! The person can be tossed as high as 30 feet (9 m) in the air. While in the air, the rider does spins, flips, or poses. He or she tries to land in a standing position. Judges look for balance, height, and midair moves.

Once he's up in the air, the blanket rider does gymnastic moves.

Glossary

endurance—ability to do something for a long time

kilt—a short, plaid, pleated skirt often worn by men in Scotland

limber—to stretch or loosen up

pin—in wrestling, to hold your opponent to the mat until time is called

Web Sites

For links to learn more about weird sports: **childsworld.com/links**

Note to Parents, Teachers, and Librarians: We routinely verify our Web links to make sure they are safe and active sites. So encourage your readers to check them out!

Index